Sometimes Mommy goes to work in the city.

"Goodbye, Diari. Goodbye, Fatima. I'll see you soon," Mommy says. She blows us kisses and off she goes!

It is still dark outside. The moon is trading places with the sun.

'Good morning, Diari!" Daddy pulls back the curtains to let the sunshine in.

'Good morning, Daddy!" Today will be a great day!

On days like today, when Mommy's away, Daddies and daughters stick together.

I brush my teeth and wash my face while Daddy combs my hair.

I make my bed and find something sparkly to wear as I say my affirmations.

"I am smart and I am kind. I have a strong mind and a good heart. I love my family and my friends—

"Oh! Good morning, Fatima!"

Daddy's making our favorite breakfast: pancakes with chocolate chips and fresh whipped cream, just the way we like it.

He always asks, "Now what ingredients go into making smart and beautiful girls like you?"

On days like today, when Mommy's away, Daddies and daughters stick together.

Now, it's time for learning.
Daddy is the best teacher.

We practice counting.

We review our sight words.

We take turns reading our best-loved books.

We learn new languages.

"Fatima, can you say *azul*?
That's blue in Spanish.

"Can you say *jaaja*?
That's big sister in Fula.

"Can you say *lapin*?
That's bunny in French."

Daddy says, "My girls are the smartest. You are learning to speak three new languages. I am so proud of you, and I love you so much!"

Then comes the best part of the day: playtime!

I pretend to be Mommy.

We run and jump and dance and touch our toes.

We stretch into our yoga poses.

After a quick lunch, it's time for a nap! Fatima loves naps, especially when she has TeeTee the Pacifier and me to keep her company.

Uh-oh! We can't find Fatima's pacifier.

"Daddy, where is Fatima's TeeTee?"

Is it under the bed? Noooo!

Is it in the closet? Noooo!

Is it in the kitchen?

Daddy wishes us sweet dreams.

When Fatima and I wake up, it's time to find Daddy.

"Daddy, where are you?"

He's making dinner.

Mmm, yummy! Daddy is cooking *thiep* (chep), our family's fried rice specialty.

As he stirs, he says, "On days like today, when mommies are away, daddies and daughters stick together!"

Daddy always asks, "Now, Diari and Fatima, what ingredients go into making healthy and strong girls like you?"

I say, "Oodles of veggies, a big cup of water, teaspoons of treats, and a ton of play!"

"Don't forget lots and lots of hugs and kisses," Daddy reminds us.

When we finish our dinner with Daddy, it's bath time, and I'm a little tired.

Today was such a great day! And it always gets better when we hear . . .

"Hello, Diari! Hi, Fatima!"

It is dark outside. The sun is trading places with the moon.

I brush my teeth, and then Mommy combs my hair.

I say my affirmations, and then we all say our prayers.

It's bedtime.

Mommy and Daddy hug us tight and tell us good night.

On nights like tonight, I'm happy to say: Mommy, Daddy, and daughters stick together.

The next book in the Daddies and Daughters series is coming soon!

Copyright © 2022 by Aissatou Balde
Illustrations © 2022 by Nandi L. Fernandez
All rights reserved.

Produced and published by Bird Upstairs, an imprint of Girl Friday Books, in association with Daddies and Daughters Co.

Published by Bird Upstairs Books™, Seattle
www.birdupstairs.com

Produced by Girl Friday Productions

Design: Paul Barrett
Development & editorial: Tegan Tigani
Production editorial: Bethany Davis
Project management: Reshma Kooner

ISBN (hardcover): 978-1-954854-52-9
Library of Congress Control Number: 2021925550

First edition
Printed in Canada

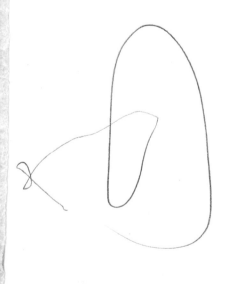